More Shakespeare Without the Boring Bits

HUMPHREY CARPENTER

More
Shakespeare Without
the Boring Bits

Illustrated by The Big i

VIKING

VIKING

Published by the Penguin Group
Penguin Books Ltd, 27 Wrights Lane, London W8 5TZ, England
Penguin Books USA Inc., 375 Hudson Street, New York, New York 10014, USA
Penguin Books Australia Ltd, Ringwood, Victoria, Australia
Penguin Books Canada Ltd, 10 Alcorn Avenue, Toronto, Ontario, Canada M4V 3B2
Penguin Books (NZ) Ltd, 182–190 Wairau Road, Auckland 10, New Zealand

Penguin Books Ltd, Registered Offices: Harmondsworth, Middlesex, England

First published 1997
3 5 7 9 10 8 6 4 2

Typeset in Monotype Janson by
Rowland Phototypesetting Ltd,
Bury St Edmunds, Suffolk
Printed in England by Clays Ltd, St Ives plc

A CIP catalogue record for this book is available from the British Library

ISBN 0–670–87201–6

Contents

Introduction

Some people were rather shocked when I wrote the first volume of *Shakespeare Without the Boring Bits*. 'There aren't any boring bits in Shakespeare,' they said to me crossly. But the fact is, there are. Lots of the jokes, for example, just aren't funny any more. They were mostly about things that were happening in Shakespeare's day, and you have to read lots of footnotes to understand them, and frankly they aren't terribly funny even then. Gags weren't Shakespeare's strongest point.

Then there are all the historical bits – all the minor dukes and earls and courtiers who wander around the stage and are given the odd line or two. I suppose Shakespeare was writing for quite a big company of actors, and he had to give them all something to do. But you can perform the main story of most of his plays with just half a dozen actors, leaving out all those bits.

Even if you agree that some lines or even whole scenes are boring, you may be one of those people who says, 'You can't rewrite Shakespeare because you lose all the poetry.' Well, of course you do. But maybe you can add something of your own. Shakespeare was writing for his own times – for the kind of people who came to the theatre 400 years ago. This book, like the first one, tackles each play by imagining how Shakespeare might have treated the story if he was writing it for us today. And if that idea disgusts you and you want to go off and read his original plays instead, that's fine! These books aren't meant to take the place of the plays. They're meant to show you that Shakespeare is exciting and *not* boring. And maybe they will encourage you to write your own versions of the plays, which could be completely different from mine.

As in the first volume, most of the stories of the plays are told by a particular character from them and the settings have usually been modernized. Recent films and productions of the plays have helped me with ideas. Having watched the 1996 film of *Othello*, with Kenneth Branagh as Iago, I feel (as a lot of people have felt about this play over the centuries) that this crucial character doesn't really make sense. *Why* should he be so determined to destroy Othello and Desdemona? Thinking about this suggested to me a new way of approaching the play. Ian McKellen's *Richard III* (also 1996) turned Richard into a Fascist dictator of the 1930s, and highlighted the First Murderer, which gave me the idea of making that character the narrator – but I changed the setting.

Tom Stoppard's *Rosencrantz and Guildenstern Are Dead*, revived at the National Theatre (again in 1996), suggested to me that my narrator for *Hamlet* could be the Player Queen – the boy actor whom Stoppard calls Alfred. But then I found myself talking to someone who had nearly remarried soon after the death of her husband, and had found her son behaving just like Hamlet. So I decided to concentrate on that aspect of the play: Hamlet's anguish not so much at the supposed murder of his father but at the fact that another man has displaced his father (an experience which quite a few teenagers go through).

Much Ado About Nothing looked tricky. How was I to handle its odd mixture of farce and tragedy? Then I remembered a recent film (not Shakespeare) which had just the same tone. Thank you, Richard Curtis, who wrote it, and Hugh Grant, who starred in it, for inspiring what I've written.

King Lear, however, *was* tricky; the sheer horror of it makes it very difficult to treat in the lightish manner of this book. But *Antony and Cleopatra* was a hoot – I knew that Cleopatra was going to be a lookalike of Madonna even before I reread the play. A little tabloid journalism didn't seem amiss here.

The Winter's Tale is in many ways a sad play, but it has its richly comic side – I can imagine Shakespeare laughing as he wrote the famous stage direction 'Exit, pursued by a bear' – and I couldn't resist opting for the comedy.

As You Like It has always seemed to me a rather irritating play, with its relentless jollity and endless pretty little songs. Then I realized that it reminded me of *Salad Days*, the 1954 musical by Julian Slade and Dorothy Reynolds, which has exactly the same undergraduate air. So my *Arden Days* is dedicated to Julian (a friend of mine), who in his own salad days wrote music for Shakespeare productions at the Bristol Old Vic.

And if anyone wants to set *Arden Days* to music, please send me a tape!

Humphrey Carpenter

Much Ado About Nothing

Opening titles: 'TWO WEDDINGS AND A FUNERAL, Written, produced and directed by William Shakespeare'

Close-up of alarm clock. It rings. Camera pans to a beautiful dark-haired young woman, Hero, asleep in bed, in a rather grand bedroom. She wakes, switches off the alarm, leaps happily out of bed and runs across the room. A superb wedding dress is on a stand next to a full-length mirror. She takes it off the stand and starts to put it on.

Cut to close-up of another alarm clock, which rings too. Camera pans to another young woman, Beatrice, in her own bed in another room in the same house. She has spiky red hair, and when she wakes she puts on a pair of heavy-rimmed glasses before reaching for the clock and switching off the alarm. She gets out of bed and goes into Hero's room. Hero is fastening up the wedding dress.

HERO:

Morning, Beatrice. Don't I look wonderful?

BEATRICE:

Frankly, Hero darling, you look like an enormous meringue.

(Close-up of a third alarm clock. This one is in Claudio's room, in another, much less grand, house. It rings. But he's up already, pacing his room in his pyjamas, biting his nails. He is dark-haired and bronzed, as dishy as a male model. He goes to the phone, dials a number, then thinks better of it and puts the receiver down.

Close-up of a fourth alarm clock. It rings for ages.

Finally Benedick, who is good-looking with mousy hair but has a silly-ass manner, wakes, stares at the clock, can't believe what he sees, swears a great deal, leaps out of bed and tries to find his clothes in his shambolic bedroom.

Interior of a marquee. Leonato, an elderly grey-haired man who is smartly dressed for the wedding in a morning suit, is checking that his staff are laying the tables correctly for the reception. He smiles at one of them, Margaret, who is arranging a big floral display.)

LEONATO:

Weather looks promising, Margaret. Shouldn't you be helping my daughter to dress?

MARGARET:

I would have, sir, but Miss Hero said to leave Miss Beatrice to do it. Miss Beatrice's tongue is as sharp as ever, sir, but I reckon she's as excited as if she was getting married herself.

LEONATO (*sighing*):
That'll be the day. Where on earth are we going to find a man who would marry my crazy niece?

MARGARET:
She likes that Mr Benedick, the best man.

LEONATO:
Does she? She's always incredibly rude about him when anyone mentions him. She says he's a complete idiot who's always in a total mess.

> (*Cut to suburban street. Benedick, in shirt and braces, is trying to start his car. It won't start. He swears a great deal.*
>
> *Cut to Hero's bedroom. Hero is in the wedding dress and Beatrice, who has a mouthful of pins, is adjusting it.*)

HERO:
I'm so glad Claudio has chosen Benedick to be best man.

BEATRICE (*through the pins*):
Well, I'm not.

HERO:
Oh, come on, he's gorgeous. Everyone says you fancy him.

BEATRICE:

Don't talk drivel. He looks like a lumpy pillow. And that beard of his is ridiculous.

HERO:

He hasn't got a beard any more. He's shaved it off for the wedding.

BEATRICE:

Then I bet he looks even worse.

(Cut to Claudio, in the bedroom of his house. Now dressed in his wedding clothes, he is sitting miserably on his bed, with his head in his hands.)

CLAUDIO *(to himself)*:

What the hell am I going to do? 'Till death us do part.' And I *saw* her . . .

(The doorbell rings. Claudio runs downstairs and opens the front door. It is Benedick.)

BENEDICK:

What ho, sorry I'm late.

CLAUDIO:
Are you? I wish you'd never come at all.

BENEDICK:
I say, old beansprout, that's not the right attitude on your wedding day.

(Cut to Margaret in the marquee, still arranging the flowers. She yawns. Leonato is fussing about.)

LEONATO:
Is the champagne all on ice? And the salmon mayonnaise all made?

MARGARET:
Yes, sir. *(She yawns again.)*

LEONATO:
Been having some late nights, Margaret? Up late with that boyfriend of yours, eh?

(Margaret giggles.

Cut to interior of pub. Borachio, a young man in a shiny suit, is drinking in a secluded corner of the bar with Don John, a rough-looking biker in heavy leathers.)

DON JOHN:
It all went smoothly?

BORACHIO:
Sure. Margaret, my girlfriend, thought it was just a bit of a giggle.

DON JOHN:
You didn't tell her what it was for?

BORACHIO:
What do you think I am?

(Cut to interior of Benedick's car, driving along a suburban street. Claudio is in the passenger seat, looking miserable.)

BENEDICK:
Oh, come on, laddie, it'll soon be over. Mind you, I'd feel pretty terrible myself if I was getting married. *Married.* The word's got a smell like yesterday's socks. You'll never catch *me* splicing the old marital knot ... Which house is Pedro's?

CLAUDIO (*gloomily*):
He's waiting for us over there.

(*The car draws up alongside Don Pedro, a plump, jolly man with a red face and beard, in an absurdly flowery waistcoat, waiting irritably on the pavement.*)

DON PEDRO:
My dear Ben, I've been standing here for about three days. Do you realize how late we are?

(*He gets into the back and they drive off at breakneck speed.*)

BENEDICK (*as he drives*):
Not my fault at all. Claudio kept me hanging about... Do you think that awful woman Beatrice will be there?

DON PEDRO:
Hero's cousin? Bound to be. She lives there.

BENEDICK:
Awful woman. Incredibly rude.

DON PEDRO:
Is she? Well, my dear Ben, everyone says she fancies you.

(*Nudges Claudio, who manages a weak smile.*)

BENEDICK (*appalled*):
What?

DON PEDRO:
Oh, yes, she's really got the hots for you, Ben, you lucky fellow. She sits up all night writing you passionate letters, but she tears them up because she's convinced you can't stand her.

BENEDICK:
Dead right I can't ... (*But he looks thoughtful as he drives.*) Any idea what's in these bally letters?

(*Cut to Hero's bedroom. Beatrice is doing Hero's hair.*)

HERO (*smiling craftily*):
Everyone knows he fancies *you*.

BEATRICE:

Benedick? Oh, *yuck*. You're not serious, are you? He's about as appealing as a pig's buttock.

(The door opens and Margaret comes in.)

MARGARET:

Excuse me, miss, are you sure there's nothing I can do?

HERO:

Isn't it true, Margaret, that Claudio's friend Benedick, the best man, is head over heels in love with Beatrice?

(She winks at Margaret, who gets the point.)

MARGARET:

Oh yes, miss, weeping his eyes out, he was, after the rehearsal for the wedding. Said he wished it was him getting married to you. He's been secretly in love with you for years.

BEATRICE:

Jeepers. Well, keep him away from me today. I

can't *stand* him ... (*But she, too, looks thoughtful.*)
You mean, really crying, was he?

MARGARET:
Oh, yes, miss, buckets. (*She giggles.*)

(*Hero's eye is caught by a cigarette end on the floor near the window.*)

HERO:
Margaret, someone's been smoking in here.

(*Margaret, spotting the cigarette end, picks it up, looking embarrassed.*)

MARGARET:
Can't think who, miss.

HERO:
That boyfriend of yours, Borachio, he smokes, doesn't he?

MARGARET (*very embarrassed*):
Yes, miss, now and then. Excuse me, miss, I must go and finish the flowers. (*She scuttles off.*)

(Cut to Borachio in the pub, lighting a cigarette.)

BORACHIO:
Where's the money, then?

DON JOHN:
What money?

BORACHIO:
You told me fifty quid. That was the price for doing it.

(Cut to exterior of pub. Silly music. Constable Dogberry, the village policeman, rides up on his bike. There is an open window right by him, and Don John's and Borachio's voices can be heard.)

DON JOHN:
Just a joke. I haven't got fifty quid.

BORACHIO:
Joke? Look, you could have got me into real trouble. And Margaret. What the hell's it all about, anyway?

(Constable Dogberry gets off his bike, pauses and listens. He scratches his head and gets out his notebook.

Cut to car park in front of village church. The bells are pealing noisily. Organ music from inside the church. A Rolls-Royce pulls up sedately, and Leonato gets out and opens the door. Hero, looking wonderful in her wedding dress, steps out of the car, followed by Beatrice, in an enormous yellow hat with cherries. Leonato gives Hero his arm and they start to walk towards the church.

Suddenly Benedick's car screeches into the car park and scrapes to a halt, knocking down a fence. Claudio and Don Pedro get out and run into the church, overtaking the bride and her father. Benedick follows them, then halts abruptly, patting his pockets.)

BENEDICK:
The ring! Where the heck —?

(He turns and tears back to the car, bumping headlong into Beatrice and knocking off her hat. He speaks, not realizing who it is.)

Oh, gosh, frightfully tremendously sorry – (*Recognising her*:) Aha. Yes. Well, er. Nice weather.

BEATRICE (*furious*):
Idiot. Look what you've done to my hat. (*She picks it up and sorts it out, but then she takes a sidelong look at him.*) Definitely better without the beard.

BENEDICK (*eating one of the cherries*):
Aren't weddings awful?

BEATRICE:
Don't talk rubbish. They're great.

BENEDICK:
Well, I mean, other people's are all right, I suppose. But you wouldn't catch me having one of my own. Not for anything.

BEATRICE (*eating a cherry*):
Nor me.

(*Interior of the church. Hero, on her father's arm, is walking up the aisle, while Don Pedro is shown to his seat. There's an empty seat next to him. He notices it's empty and looks puzzled.*

Interior of the pub. Don John is rather drunk now.)

BORACHIO:
Shouldn't you be at the wedding?

DON JOHN:
There isn't going to be a wedding, not after what you've done. Anyway, I don't want to sit next to that appalling half-brother of mine.

BORACHIO:
Don Pedro? What's wrong with him? That was how Hero met Claudio, him being a friend of Don Pedro.

DON JOHN:
Exactly. Pedro and his stupid stuck-up friends. I'm sick of them all. That's why I set up this hoax, to mess up their wonderful wedding get-together.

(Exterior of pub. Constable Dogberry, who has been

listening to this, nods to himself and snaps his notebook shut.)

CONSTABLE DOGBERRY (*meaningfully*):
Aha. Aha. *Aha.*

(Interior of church. Claudio and Hero are standing in front of the Vicar.)

VICAR:
We are here today to join in holy matrimony these two young people. (*Whispering to Claudio:*) Where's the best man?

(Claudio turns round. There is no sign of Benedick.

Cut to the churchyard. Benedick and Beatrice are finishing the cherries.)

BENEDICK:
I mean, think of being married to someone. Just think of what it would be like.

BEATRICE:
Absolutely dreadful.

BENEDICK:

You know, you're the first person I've ever met who feels the same way about it. (*Gazing into her eyes.*) Isn't that an interesting coincidence?

BEATRICE (*gazing earnestly back*):
Oh, yes. *Yes.*

(*There is a deafening whistle and a shout of 'Hoi!'. Don Pedro, at the church doorway, is beckoning frantically to Benedick.*

Inside the church:)

VICAR:

If any of you know any good reason why this man and this woman should not be joined together in holy matrimony, then speak now ... Claudio, do you take this –

(*But Claudio is clearing his throat.*)

CLAUDIO (*loudly*):
Er, I'm afraid I *do* know why she shouldn't. Because she's nothing but a cheap tart.

(Alarm and dismay among the wedding guests.)

You see, I was sent an anonymous note telling me to take a walk in Hero's father's garden last night, and I did, and I looked up to her window, and there she was, hugging and kissing some other man. And he kept sighing 'Oh, Hero!' and she was snogging him like blazes. So I'm afraid I'm not going to go ahead with this.

(Hero gasps and collapses on to the church floor. Screams of horror from the congregation. Close-up of Margaret looking very guilty. Total mayhem — just as Benedick comes into the church.

Cut to the village street. Constable Dogberry is leading Don John and Borachio, handcuffed to each other, as he pushes his bike.)

CONSTABLE DOGBERRY:
I know exactly what you've been up to, my lads. You're plotting to bring down the British government.

(An ambulance with siren and flashing lights appears

22

almost from nowhere and nearly knocks them all down as it roars past.

Inside the church, Benedick is staring at Leonato and Don Pedro.)

BENEDICK:
I've never heard so much rubbish in my life. Old Claudio's completely off his nut. She's no tart. She hasn't got eyes for any man except him. Anyone can see that.

(Claudio is sitting with his head in his hands. Two Ambulance Men hurry in and lift Hero on to a stretcher. Beatrice storms up to Benedick.)

BEATRICE:
Well, don't just stand there, *do* something.

BENEDICK:
Um, I could hit Claudio if you like? Actually I don't think that would help a frightful lot.

DON PEDRO:
I'm sure my poisonous half-brother is behind this.

He's always trying to mess up anything I'm involved in.

BENEDICK:
Oh, do come on, let's get her to the ambulance. (*He follows the stretcher out of the church, to the ambulance.*)

   (*Close-up of stretcher. Hero opens her eyes.*)

HERO:
Where am I?

BENEDICK:
Phew! I really thought you'd had it, old strawberry. (*An idea strikes him. He whispers to her.*) Shut them again. Play dead.

   (*She shuts her eyes. Beatrice runs up.*)

BEATRICE:
Is she going to be all right?

BENEDICK:
Yes, but for goodness' sake don't tell a ruddy soul. Inspector Benedick is on the case.

Much Ado About Nothing

(Interior of the church. Claudio is still sitting with his head in his hands. The Vicar is trying to comfort Leonato, who keeps shaking his head and looks desperate. Benedick rushes in and whispers to Leonato, who looks astonished at first, then nods. Benedick then whispers to the Vicar, who nods too.)

VICAR *(to the wedding guests)*:
Please can I have everyone's attention? A tragedy has occurred. I'm very, very sorry to have to tell you that Hero has died of grief.

(A groan from everyone. Claudio collapses in misery.)

We were going to have a wedding, but I'm afraid it's going to have to be a funeral instead.

(The organist begins to play sad music. Constable Dogberry stomps into the church, still with his bicycle and his prisoners.)

CONSTABLE DOGBERRY:
Begging your pardon, ladies and gentlemen, but does anyone have one of them mobile phones? I need to make an urgent call to the Prime Minister.

(A gasp from Margaret as she sees Borachio.)

MARGARET:
Borachio! You never told me what it was for, you
lying –

BENEDICK (*his eyes opening wide*):
Wait a minute! I say, Margaret, could it possibly
have been *you* at that window last night?

MARGARET (*tearfully*):
He kept calling me by Miss Hero's name. I
thought it were just a joke.

CONSTABLE DOGBERRY (*proudly*):
I have apprehended these two terrorists under the
Defence of the Realm Act.

DON JOHN:
You halfwit copper, let us go.

DON PEDRO:
I thought so. My trouble-making half-brother.
You were behind it, weren't you?

(Don John nods.)

BENEDICK:
Gosh, well, that's a happy ending.

CLAUDIO:
No, it isn't. Hero is dead.

BENEDICK:
Yes, and it was all your fault for jumping to conclusions. Which is why you'd better agree to marry her lookalike cousin. (*He points to the back of the church.*)

(Everyone turns round. Hero, fully recovered, is standing in the church doorway. Everyone cheers.)

In fact, Vicar, I think it had better be a double. Would you mind marrying Beatrice and me?

BEATRICE:
What! You might have asked me, you rat.

BENEDICK:

Oh, yes, sorry, Beatrice, old thingummy. Don't mind, do you?

BEATRICE:

Absolute cheek. But I suppose I'd better take pity on you, since you've been pining away for me for so many years. All that weeping.

BENEDICK:

Wait a tick. I thought *you* were the one who was pining for *me*. All those letters.

BEATRICE:

Letters? What letters?

VICAR:

Never mind. I'm sure you'll both be very happy together. Two weddings coming right up!

(Everyone cheers. Closing titles.)

Hamlet

TOLD BY HAMLET AND OPHELIA

THURSDAY

The worst day of my life.

Until now, the worst day was when Dad died.
But this is worse.

I came home to find that Mum has got married
again. And to Uncle Claudius, for God's sake.

I'm feeling too sick to write anything more.

*   *   *

Monday

The sight of Uncle Claudius touching Dad's things, his books, his clothes – he's even wearing some of them – and, worst of all, *touching Mum* makes me want to throw up. Worse than that, it makes me want to kill Uncle Claudius.

Oh, God, I wish I was dead.

*   *   *

Sunday

I'm so miserable. I was so looking forward to Hamlet coming back home at the end of his university term, but now he's here and it's awful. He won't even look at me. And Laertes keeps saying to me, 'I told you so, Ophelia. He never really loved you at all. He was just fooling around with you.' Which of course just makes me run up to my room and lock the door and cry my heart out. Brothers are awful. I wish Laertes would go away to university and never come back in the holidays.

Pa is trying to persuade me that Hamlet doesn't mean to be cruel to me at all. 'He's so desperately in love with you,' Pa says, 'that he's terrified of even looking at you, let alone talking to you. You should be flattered.'

It's kind of Pa, but it doesn't make sense. Hamlet wasn't like that at Christmas, not even in January, when his father died so suddenly. He was terribly upset, but he used to talk to me about it, and he'd let me hug him and make it better. And he ought to be happier now that dear old Claudius has married Gertrude. It's much better for him to have a stepfather than no father at all. And who could be a better stepfather than his uncle?

* * *

TUESDAY

The best day of my life.

Something absolutely incredible has happened.

I went to bed early, so I wouldn't have to watch *them* hugging and kissing in front of the telly. It make me want to throw things at them. Or worse.

As I was going upstairs, I ran into Ophelia. Poor kid, she looked at me so pathetically. I *wish* I could still fancy her, the way I used to. And it was more than fancying. I was in love with her,

I really was. But now all that's gone dead in me. I couldn't love anyone now, not ever again. I don't feel hungry, I don't feel thirsty, I don't feel tired, I can't feel excited about anything. I'm just dead all through, except for the one red-hot glowing bit of me, which is hatred of Uncle Claudius for pretending he can step into Dad's shoes – he was literally wearing a pair of his shoes today, the swine. And hatred of Mum for marrying him – my God, it's still not two months since Dad died.

So I just pushed past Ophelia on the stairs and said nothing. I could hear her crying as she went down.

I got to my room and slammed the door, and locked it, and threw myself on to my bed.

I must have fallen asleep, because the next thing I knew it was very, very dark and quiet, and I was cold and shivering. And in the distance, I could hear the phone ringing.

It rang on and on and on. That was very odd, because there are phones all over the house, and someone usually answers it after a few rings, and anyway there's an answering machine which cuts in pretty quickly.

But now it was just ringing and ringing and ringing.

So in the end, I got off my bed, unlocked the door and went downstairs.

It was the phone in the hall. All the lights were off and the grandfather clock said it was three o'clock, which must have meant three in the morning, and the phone went on ringing and ringing.

So I picked it up.

'Hello,' said a voice. 'It's me.'

There's only one person who says 'It's me' when he rings up.

Dad.

And he's dead.

I gripped the phone hard. 'Who's that?' I said.

'Who do you think?' laughed Dad's voice. It was him all right.

'Dad!' I shouted. 'You're all right! I don't believe it!'

'Quiet,' said Dad. 'We don't want everyone to hear. Yes, I'm all right, in a manner of speaking.'

'Where are you? When can I see you? I must see you now!'

'Sorry, Hamlet old thing,' said Dad. 'You can't.

Not for the time being anyway. And there's something I want you to do.'

'Anything, Dad, you know that. Just tell me.'

'Kill your uncle.'

'*What?*'

'You heard me, Hamlet. Kill your uncle. Because he killed me.'

* * *

WEDNESDAY

Gertrude had a long talk with me this morning. She's very worried about Hamlet and so am I. He barged past me on the stairs last night as if I didn't exist, and this morning he looks as if he's seen a ghost.

I found him in the hall just after breakfast, taking the telephone to pieces with a screwdriver. His clothes were all in a terrible mess — he must have dressed with his eyes shut. 'I must make sure it isn't a trick,' he kept muttering. When I asked him what he was doing, he said, 'Do you think dead people can make phone calls, Ophelia?'

I was quite pleased that he'd actually spoken to me at last, but he sounded completely crazy and his eyes were wild, so I was rather frightened, and ran off and told Gertrude.

She's been like a mother to me ever since my own mother died and Pa and Laertes and I came to live with Hamlet and his parents. And now she was terribly kind and understanding.

'You know we've always hoped that you would marry Hamlet,' she said. 'But he's been terribly cut up by his father's death. I thought he would get better, now that Claudius can be a second father to him, but I'm afraid he's going through a very difficult stage. This morning he rushed into our bedroom when Claudius and I were dressing and demanded to know what exactly it was his father had died of. As if he didn't know already!'

'It was a wasp sting, wasn't it?' I said.

'Yes, dear. He'd been sitting in the garden and unfortunately he was terribly allergic to stings, and when this one got him he just blew up like a balloon and died in hospital. But this morning Hamlet was muttering something about poisons, and he even started going through the medicine cupboard in our bathroom. I'm really very worried about him.'

'Me too,' I said.

Just then Pa came in.

'Polonius, dear,' said Gertrude to him, 'do sit down. You look quite exhausted.'

My father sat and mopped his brow. 'I've just been helping the actors put up their scenery,' he said. 'It looks splendid.'

Gertrude frowned. 'I really wonder whether we should be having the play tonight,' she said, 'with Hamlet in such a state.'

Pa smiled. 'Oh, don't worry about him,' he said. 'He's having a fine old time. He's giving the actors a lesson in acting!'

* * *

WEDNESDAY

I couldn't believe it at first. Not only has Mum behaved appallingly by getting married again so soon after my father's death – and to *him* – she's also shown the most unbelievable lack of taste.

Dad always used to invite some old college friends to perform a play at our house one weekend every spring. They'd put it on in the barn and we'd invite all the local people to come and watch.

And would you believe it, she's invited them

again this year, so soon after Dad's death – and they're going to put on a thriller, a murder mystery. Have you ever heard of anything so tasteless?

But I've had a brilliant idea.

I've written an extra scene for the play. *Showing how Dad really died.* And I've persuaded them to add it to their script.

I didn't tell them why I wanted them to add it, of course. I didn't explain it was about Dad and Uncle Claudius and Mum. I just said there were some local jokes in it which the audience would enjoy.

I was talking to the actors when Ophelia's father barged in, the interfering old busybody. I wasn't going to tell *him* what was going on, of course.

There's just an hour to curtain-up.

*   *   *

WEDNESDAY – VERY LATE

What an awful evening.

Hamlet made me sit by him at the play, and he even held my hand when the houselights were switched off, but he seemed incredibly tense and he soon let go of it.

At first I thought it was just the usual corny old country-house murder-mystery stuff, with a butler who kept answering the phone, and the village spinster busybody, a comic vicar and a doctor who was the worse for drink. But then came a scene which was quite different.

The country house was the home of a duke and duchess, and the duchess was having an affair behind her husband's back. We knew that from the beginning of the play, but now it turned out that the person she was having the affair with was her husband's brother. Well, this was a bit embarrassing for the audience, though no one has ever suggested that Gertrude was having an affair with Claudius before the awful tragedy of the wasp sting.

But there was worse to come. We saw the duke sitting down in a deck chair in the garden, reading the paper and then falling asleep, whereupon his brother crept in and injected him with a syringe, and he got up, screaming, and then fell down dead. And then the brother told everyone he'd died of a wasp sting.

Well, the play had got to this point when Claudius stood up and said, 'This must stop. I think we'd better have the lights on again.' He was quite calm about it, but everyone could see that he and Gertrude were terribly upset.

But Hamlet laughed and laughed and laughed.

*   *   *

WEDNESDAY – MIDNIGHT

I'm waiting for the phone to ring, and for Dad to tell me how well I did.

I *proved* that Uncle Claudius killed him. I really did. You could *see* it in Uncle Claudius's face when he stood up and had the lights put on.

He was white as a sheet and shaking. And Mum looked as if she'd been found out at last.

I've proved that they're guilty, in front of everyone! And I should have killed Uncle Claudius then and there. God knows how. I've never killed anyone, and I don't think I'd ever have the nerve to do it.

But I've got to. It's what Dad told me to do.

Oh, why doesn't the phone ring again?

I couldn't have *dreamt* that Dad rang up, could I?

*   *   *

THURSDAY

I have killed him.
But it wasn't the right him.
It was —

*　　*　　*

THURSDAY

I shall go mad.
Hamlet has killed Pa.
I shall —

*　　*　　*

THURSDAY

Mum still hasn't rung the police. I don't know why. They must take me away and do their worst with me. I have killed the wrong person.

The morning after the play, Mum asked me to come to her sitting room. She said she badly needed to talk to me. She wanted to know why I had spoilt the play, and whether I really believed that Uncle Claudius had killed Dad.

So I told her that Dad had telephoned me and said so. I thought that would make her understand. But she looked at me as if I was completely mad.

It was then that I heard the sneeze. Someone was hiding behind the curtains.

Without thinking, I snatched up a paperknife from Mum's desk and jabbed it at the curtains. The person behind the curtains yelled out. A man's voice. *Him.* My chance at last. So I began to stab seriously. I plunged and jabbed and *pushed* with the paperknife.

There were some awful noises and red stains started to come through the curtains. Mum tried to pull me away, but I hit at her and went on stabbing.

Then *he* went limp and fell down, and there was silence.

I pulled the curtains open.

It wasn't Uncle Claudius. It was Ophelia's old busybody father.

What have I done? What is to happen?

And still the phone doesn't ring.

*   *   *

FRIDAY

Ophelia was found dead this morning in the swimming pool.

Mum still doesn't call the police.

Ophelia's brother is roaming the house, looking for me.

Well, I'm ready for him.

And I'll get Uncle Claudius too.

*   *   *

HOUSE OF HORROR
**Multiple slayings at Elsinore Manor
Family squabble that ended in tragedy
'No survivors,' say police**

First reports of the slaughter at Elsinore Manor, near Copenhagen, suggest that an entire household has been wiped out in a series of revenge killings. A local resident whose suspicions had been aroused by screams and shouts describes 'piles of corpses'. We hope to bring you further details in our next edition.

Antony and Cleopatra

THE POLITICIAN AND
THE POP SINGER
Foreign Minister in Super-Yacht Scandal

A Daily Moon *Exclusive*

The *Moon* can reveal that Italian foreign minister, Mark Antony, is having a torrid relationship with world-famous Egyptian pop singer Cleopatra.

Tanned and handsome Mark Antony flew to Egypt on Monday morning, to take part in Middle

East peace negotiations. But he never arrived at the conference table.

36-year-old Mark is happily married. His wealthy wife, Fulvia, is one of the top women in Rome society. But, like millions of other people worldwide, he's a passionate fan of Cleopatra. And it seems he was desperate to meet the fabulously rich, famously sexy singer.

Armed with Cleo's closely guarded phone number, he dialled her secret hideout.

Cleopatra, whose outrageously sexy records and videos have made her notorious around the globe, decided she liked the sound of his voice. She set sail down the Nile for Alexandria in her stupendous yacht *Sphinx.*

The multi-million-dollar boat is one of the most costly private yachts ever built. Incredibly, its hull and superstructure are plated with 22-carat gold.

A crowd of more than 10,000 people were on Alexandria dockside to watch the arrival of *Sphinx.* And they got a noseful as well as an eyeful! Because the boat's purple sails are regularly drenched in thousands of dollars' worth of Chanel perfume!

Immediately *Sphinx* cast anchor, the scantily dressed superstar pulled another sexy trick. She was rowed across to the quay in a boat that was even more stunning than the yacht – silver oars, a cloth-of-gold canopy and even a guitarist to serenade her with her own hits. The oarsmen rowed in time with the music. And to keep Cleo cool in the evening heat, a tanned young man dressed as Cupid waved a giant fan.

Onlookers say Mark Antony was bowled over by the stunning display the superstar had staged for him.

The crowd cheered as Cleo's boat arrived. She walked slinkily up the red-carpeted steps to meet the handsome Italian politician.

Mark Antony had planned for Cleo to dine with him in his luxury hotel suite. He'd ordered a lavish champagne dinner. But Cleo had decided *she'd* be the host. And onlookers could see that Mark Antony needed no persuasion to come on board the *Sphinx*!

The pair stepped into Cleopatra's rowing boat and the Italian minister was carried off to the super-yacht. And he hasn't been seen since!

He was due to fly back to Rome on Wednesday night. But in the early hours of Tuesday, *Sphinx* slipped out of harbour. A spokesman for Mark Antony said he was taking a short holiday.

In Rome, 35-year-old Mrs Fulvia Antony told the *Moon*: 'Mark must have gone out of his wits. He collects Cleopatra's records, but that's just because he likes the music. She's a scheming bitch who wants to get involved in politics. You can tell her from me, "Give my husband back!"'

*   *   *

PASSION AMONG THE PYRAMIDS
Mystery disease strikes down wife of cheating Mark
Will Ant wed Cleo?

The Moon *is first with the story*

The sex-romp of Italian politician and sultry Egyptian super-singer was hit by tragedy yesterday. Italy's foreign minister, Mark Antony, besieged by reporters at the sun-drenched Pyramids hideaway of megastar Cleopatra, wept as he was told by a *Moon* reporter that his wife had died suddenly of a mystery illness.

'This is terrible,' he sobbed. 'Fulvia was a good woman.' Asked if he had been cheating on her, the 36-year-old politico, bronzed and clad in designer beachwear, replied: 'A man can love two women.'

Italy has been rocked by secretly filmed videos of the politico and the queen of pop, as they romped at Cleopatra's gold-plated swimming pool, in the shade of Egypt's massive Pyramids.

One sequence shows Mark Antony fishing in the pool. He impresses Cleo by catching a giant shark – though the camera reveals that, seconds earlier, a cunningly hidden diver had placed the big fish (conveniently dead and stuffed) on the end of his line.

Another shot reveals Mark clowning naughtily in Cleo's lace undies. Foreign office spokesmen in Rome are furiously denying that the pictures are authentic. But privately sources admit that the government is in deep trouble over the affair. 'If

Antony doesn't get back here fast and explain himself,' said one high-level source, 'we could be facing a real crisis.'

Meanwhile, Cleo has made no secret of her hopes to wed Mark Antony. 'We were made for each other,' she told the *Moon.*

*   *   *

CLEO: 'I'LL KILL HIM!'
Jilted superstar beats up *Moon* reporter Mark Antony's 'change of mind'

by Kelvin McBeth, the Moon's *man in Egypt*

Egyptian pop queen Cleopatra today made a murderous attack on me, though the real object of her fury was her Italian lover, foreign minister Mark Antony.

Only yesterday, Cleo was telling me of her plans to wed Mark (36) at a lavish open-air ceremony at the source of the Nile. Multinational TV cable and satellite corporations had opened the bidding for rights to provide live coverage of the event.

But then I was able to spring the startling news that Mark had other ideas.

Recalled to Rome by prime minister Octavius, he apparently received a severe ticking-off for his affair with the Egyptian beauty. After three hours of talks with Octavius, he emerged from government headquarters white-faced and refusing to talk to the media. Sources close to him said: 'He is having a big rethink.'

Next morning came the shock announcement. Mark Antony is to wed – but his bride won't be Cleo.

He's to marry the prime minister's 35-year-old sister, Octavia.

The news astonished Italy – and stunned Cleopatra.

'I don't believe it!' she screamed, as I broke it to her at her palatial Pyramids home.

When I assured her it was true, she picked up a knife and tried to attack me. Never in my years as a fearless newshound have I seen anyone so frantic. To coin a phrase, hell hath no fury like Cleopatra spurned.

Restrained by her staff, she broke down and wept.

'How old is this Octavia?' she sobbed. 'What colour is her hair? What's she got that I haven't got?'

When I showed her a photograph of the serious-minded 35-year-old bespectacled Italian brunette, Cleopatra burst into hysterical laughter and yelled: 'She looks about 90!'

A close friend of Octavia's confirmed: 'She's not exactly the life and soul of the party. I can't imagine what she and Mark Antony will have in common.'

The gossip in Rome government circles is that Antony has had to make this marriage to save his political career and the reputation of the government. 'Cleopatra is nothing more than a porn queen,' said one foreign office source. 'He was doing no good to Italy's image. Marrying Octavia should clean up his act.'

Cleopatra was today said to be 'under sedation' as she recovered from the news.

* * *

'IT'S TRUE LOVE!'
Antony back with Cleo
Marriage was 'a sham'
Danger of war

Kelvin McBeth on the story for the Moon

Italy is to send troops to Egypt in a bid to rescue its 'kidnapped' foreign minister, Mark Antony.

But Antony has made it clear that he fled Rome, and returned to live with rock superstar Cleopatra, of his own free will.

'She's the sexiest woman in the world,' he said tonight, giving an interview to the *Moon* on Cleopatra's giant-sized bed, which is covered with priceless mink furs.

'My marriage was a sham. Octavia's a nice person, but we hadn't a thing to say to each other.'

With a lovelorn look in his eyes, he continued: 'Cleo and I don't need words. We just gaze into each other's eyes.'

But Antony's love-idyll at Cleopatra's multi-million-dollar Pyramids home may come to a violent end. Italian soldiers have landed at Cairo airport and are on their way to snatch Antony back – if necessary, by force.

They're commanded in person by prime minister Octavius, brother of Mark Antony's abandoned wife.

'It's more than just a family quarrel,' he said tonight. 'This temptress Cleopatra is a powerful woman politically. If we don't act at once, it could be global war.'

Mark Antony has said he'll fight to the death, rather than return to Rome and his marriage. 'Cleo will fight alongside me,' he told reporters. 'She's like a devil when she's roused – and if she fights as well as she makes love, those soldiers had better take cover.'

Troops will need to take care if they get across the perimeter fence into Cleo's palatial residence. Not only are there armed security guards: Cleopatra also has a world-famous collection of poisonous snakes, which she features in her stage act.

* * *

BLOODBATH AT THE PYRAMIDS
Double suicide of politico and pop queen
'Misunderstanding' led to tragedy

McBeth of the Moon *saw it happen*

Superstar Cleopatra and political leader Antony are both dead, a shocked world learned last night.

It seems the couple committed suicide – through a tragic misunderstanding.

Yesterday afternoon Italian troops stormed Cleopatra's luxury fortress villa, in the shadow of Egypt's Pyramids. Cleo's armed bodyguards were easily overcome and the defecting Italian foreign minister was put under arrest.

Eyewitnesses said that he blamed Cleopatra for his downfall. 'I wish I'd never set eyes on you,' he screamed furiously at her, as he faced up to the fact that his political career was in ruins.

Cleo didn't stop to bandy words with her furious Italian lover. She rushed off and locked herself in her sumptuous fur-lined bedroom. And word soon came that she had killed herself.

Hearing this, Antony snatched an ancient ceremonial sword which was hanging on a wall and stabbed himself in the stomach.

A few minutes later, villa staff found that Cleopatra wasn't dead. She'd just been bluffing. However, Antony was bleeding to death.

Cleo gave orders for him to be carried up to her room. Emergency medical services were summoned and meanwhile the two lovers had much to say to each other – overheard by your *Moon* reporter, who was hiding in a cupboard.

He told her: 'I am dying, Egypt, dying.' It seems to have been one of his pet names for her.

Cleo wept as the life drained from the 36-year-old politician. But there was nothing she could do to save him. By the time emergency medical services could get there, it was all over.

And, while medicos had their backs turned, Cleo took a drastic step.

She had apparently given orders for several snakes from her reptile collection to be brought to her bedroom, hidden in a basket of figs. As I looked on, horrified, she deliberately plunged her arm into the basket and, as she had intended, received a deadly poisonous bite.

Instantly, she dropped dead in agony.

Italian prime minister Octavius, who led the military expedition, has paid tribute to the dead couple. 'Antony was one of our very best cabinet ministers,' he said. 'It's a terrible loss. And millions will mourn Cleopatra. She was truly a superstar.'

Plans are already afoot in Hollywood for a film about the life and death of the glamorous couple. 'There should be no difficulty in casting the two main roles,' said the president of the Blockbuster Film Corporation, Mr Bill Shakespeare. 'Hollywood is full of people like Antony and Cleopatra.'

Richard III

TOLD BY THE FIRST MURDERER

I'm in security. Know what I mean?

Me and my mate was on the door at a dance. Big posh ball at the palace, to tell the truth. The Yorks was having a big celebration. They'd done in the Lancasters, what had been their rivals. A lot of blood had flowed and the Lancasters was mostly in their graves now. Well, that's business, isn't it?

So the booze was really flowing. The oldest of the three York brothers, Eddie, what had made himself king now the Lancasters had got shot to pieces, was tipping it down, though he was a sick man. The middle brother, Clarry, was drinking his share too. But not the youngest, Tricky Dicky.

They were none of them beauties, but Dicky took the prize for looks. Awful looks, I mean. A lot of people called him the Toad, but some wisecracking guy said he looked like a spider trying to get out of a bottle. Spider was what I always called him, once I'd heard that.

Spider had done his bit to put the Lancasters out of the way. Him, Clarry and Eddie had taken turns to use the Lancaster king's son for target practice. But it was Spider who'd had his own little bit of fun with the king himself, old Henry Lancaster. Which is why Henry was six feet under.

I could see Spider wasn't enjoying the party. And I could guess why. He'd been to a lot of trouble for that family of his. Killed the king, no less. And where had it got him? Nowhere. His brother Eddie was the king now, the big boss, the current owner of the crown jewels, and Spider was still just Spider, the funny-looking youngest brother.

After a bit, Spider sidled up to me, clutching a champagne glass in one of his spidery hands. 'Don't I know you?' he hissed. That was his usual way of talking.

'Could be,' I grunted. 'Me and my mate has been around a bit, done a few things. Know what I mean?'

Spider looked me up and down. 'Wouldn't mind a bit of, well, *bother*, would you?'

'Depends on the terms,' I said.

Spider's voice dropped to a whisper. 'Supposing I asked you to put a friend of mine out of the way?'

'I'd rather it was two enemies,' I said, and he laughed.

'One at a time,' he hissed. 'We'll start with Clarry.'

I blinked. 'Your brother? You can't be serious.'

He nodded. 'Won't be a hard job,' he muttered. 'Clarry doesn't know it yet, but he's on his way to the Tower of London.'

I thought Spider must be off his head. Clarry was right in front of my eyes, eating and drinking his head off with the rest of them. But just at that moment Eddie, the king, rapped on the table for silence.

'Great to see you all here,' he said. 'And I have some interesting news. My horoscope says I'm to beware of someone whose name begins with "G". He's out to kill my kids. So ...' his eyes strayed to Clarry, 'I've taken a bit of advice,' and at this point he looked at Spider, 'and the advice is, to put George, Duke of Clarence, out of harm's way for the time being.' He clicked his fingers and a couple of cops dashed in, one of them with the cuffs ready. They had them on Clarry in a trice, before he knew what had happened. 'Bye-bye, Clarry,' said Eddie, 'and sleep well in the Tower.'

You see, George, Duke of Clarence was Clarry's full name. Which is how Spider had been able to persuade Eddie to lock him up. But then I remembered that Spider's full name was Richard, Duke of Gloucester. That's got a G in it too.

Next day, me and my mate wrote a letter to Spider. Well, my mate did. He's the one who's good at writing.

Your Excellency,

We has done the job what you desired of us, trust the bill (enclosed) is to your liking, terms strictly cash by the end of the month.

We had not been inside the Tower of London before except as tourists, we must say it is very smart, they really know how to look after persons what is confined there, better than what they do in Dartmoor and the Scrubs and we should know.

Your brother had got a nice set of rooms and a bathroom, more of a hotel than a prison.

He was having a bath when we arrived. We heard him saying to the screw (what you would call the jailer) that he had had a bad nightmare that you had pushed him off a ship and he was drowning.

We was able to make his dream come true right away.

Trusting everything is in order.

Yours sincerely,
       J. Dighton & P. Forrest
       Security specialists

PS Here is the videotape. Trust it has come out nicely.

Oh, yeah, I forgot to tell you, Spider gave us a camcorder and told us to film it all. The killing, I mean. Bit twisted, if you ask me, but we didn't complain. A job is a job.

*   *   *

Course it was all over the papers next day: 'ORDER OF THE BATH!' screamed the tabloids. 'The Duke of Clarence, brother to the king and third in line to the throne, was today awarded the Order of the Bath – and we don't mean the medal! His drowned body was found in a bath in the Tower of London, where he had just been imprisoned by King Edward. The Palace today issued a statement: "Although the duke was sent to the Tower by order of the king, on account of dire warnings His Majesty had received about the duke's intentions towards his sons, every care was being taken with his personal safety, and no war-rant for his execution had been issued. Police investigations are currently under way."'

Of course the papers all thought King Eddie was behind it. There were shock-horror headlines like 'HOROSCOPE WARNING – NOW CLARENCE HAS PAID THE PRICE', when the story about the letter 'G' began to get out.

But the truth was, King Eddie had been fond of Clarry and when everyone started saying he'd had him killed, he was quite upset. In fact it made his illness much worse. And a couple of months later he was dead.

My mate and I was on the door at the funeral drinks party, and I must say Spider was looking very perky, compared to the last time I saw him. But then he would, wouldn't he? With Clarry and Eddie both gone, he was two steps closer to Eddie's job. Being king, I mean.

Mind you, there remained two kids, Eddie's boys. One of them was just a little nipper, but the other – the one who was supposed to be king, now his dad was dead – was a teenager. Eddie had hid the older one away in the country, and I don't blame him. But now Spider wanted to get him into his web. (They'd given Spider the title 'Lord Protector'. Him, protect anything? That's a laugh!)

'Country air's all very well,' Spider hissed to me, 'but I reckon it's time the lad had a taste of London. What do you think, my friend?'

'They say the view is very nice from the Tower,' says I.

'Exactly,' nodded Spider, twisting his hands in a way I suppose was meant to look cheerful, though it gave me the creeps. 'And we don't want him to be lonely there, do we?' He nodded his head in the direction of Eddie's little boy, the younger one, who was eating ice cream on a chair next to his mum.

'A wink is as good as a nod,' says I, and toddled over to my mate. 'We got another job,' I told him. 'We gotter take a couple of kids for a little joy-ride.'

'Where does we put the bodies?' mumbled my mate.

'Easy, easy,' I said. 'First things first.'

But of course my mate was right. When we picked up the BMW, there was a note tucked under the windscreen, in spidery handwriting, telling us what to do. Including the video.

We collected them kids, and very nice they was, I must say. Young for their ages, mind. When we delivered them to their room in the Tower, they started having a pillow fight.

So we joined in.

I kept expecting the headlines: 'HEIRS TO THRONE IN PILLOW MYSTERY. DID KING'S SONS SMOTHER EACH OTHER IN SUICIDE PACT?' But in fact the papers never got wind of it, not till a long time after. Because all the attention was on the crowning of the new king. Yes, I mean Spider.

He did it cleverly, that last bit, make no mistake. He went on TV, to be interviewed by a smarmy newcaster called Buckingham. The whole thing was a set-up from the start, of course. It went something like this:

BUCKINGHAM:
We have with us tonight in *Newsrama* the Lord Protector of England, His Grace the Duke of Gloucester. Your Grace –

SPIDER (*oozing with false modesty*):
Just call me Dick, please.

BUCKINGHAM:
Well, er, Dick, this title 'Lord Protector' means you're virtually the king. And as I'm sure you realize, a very great number of people – perhaps the majority of citizens of this country – would like you to be just that.

SPIDER (*smarming at the camera*):
Well, of course, I'm deeply flattered and honoured by their opinion of me, but there's absolutely no

question of my accepting the throne. My brother Edward, God rest his soul, was a fine king, and if my dear brother Clarence, whose tragic death (*he dabs his eyes with his handkerchief*) has been the greatest grief of my life, had lived, he would have been a wonderful one. No, I'm thinking of becoming a clergyman and maybe going into a monastery.

There was a lot more like this, and Buckingham kept saying that the opinion polls proved that Spider would be the most popular king ever. After about half an hour, even me and my mate was getting fooled that people wanted Spider on the throne but he was too modest to accept the crown.

Spider told me that the moment they was off the air, Buckingham demanded his cash. A million, I think he said it was. Spider told him he'd pay him at midnight, fixed the spot where they was to meet.

Then he sent us along. Without the cash, of course. But with the video camera.

But Buckingham was wiser than some of them. When we got there, he'd scarpered. Not that my mate and me minded. We had plenty of other jobs from Spider. In fact we'd never worked so hard in our lives.

If you asked me how many people we handled for Spider round about this time, I'd have to say I lost count. You'd have to run the video to check the numbers. The only one me and my mate really remembers is Lord Hastings. He'd been part of the team that was putting Spider up for king, and he suddenly changed his mind. So Spider told us to put him on the list. 'Send me his head by dinner time,' he told us.

That meant it was a chainsaw job. And, would you believe it, Hastings wanted to say his prayers before we got on with it. 'Don't waste our time,' I told him. 'Spider wants his supper.'

It made a lovely video.

When Buckingham scarpered, he went off to Wales. And not for a holiday. A bloke called Henry Tudor was down there, starting a rebellion.

Spider was king now, but me and my mate could see he was worried. 'Pop down to Wales like a couple of good chaps,' he hissed at us, 'and get this Tudor creature off my back, would you?'

But we had to shake our heads. 'Too big for

us, Your Majesty,' we told him. 'He's got a lot of supporters. You'll need an army.'

Of course, being the king, he'd got an army, but armies need leaders and Spider wasn't really up to leading anybody any more – at least, not on the morning of the battle.

My mate and I had come along for the ride, to do the odd job for Spider if he needed it, and I could see there was something wrong. He was deadly pale and his hand was shaking as he tried to drink his coffee, an hour before dawn and the beginning of the fighting.

'Not slept so well, Your Majesty?' me and my mate asked him.

He shook his head. 'I shouldn't have watched the video before I went to bed.'

'The video?' we asked him.

He nodded. 'Somebody must have messed around with the tape,' he said. 'Those people who you ... dealt with for me – Clarry and the kids and Hastings and all the others – instead of ... dying, they kept leering at the camera. Pointing at me, laughing at me. And saying: "You don't stand a chance in this battle, you poor jerk. Not a chance!"'

'You're imagining things,' we told him. 'We was there. They just lay down and died, quietly like.' But we couldn't make him cheer up.

He lost the battle, of course. The last time me and my mate saw him, he was screaming for transport to get him out of difficulties. 'Even a horse would do!' he yelled.

Me and my mate could have picked him up in the BMW. But we was making ourselves scarce. Heading back for London. To be ready for the next king, Henry Tudor – Henry VII as he calls himself now.

Well, he's bound to need us sooner or later. They all do.

Othello

TOLD BY OTHELLO

1 JANUARY

We've done it! Desdemona and I got married secretly this evening, and her pa didn't know a thing until it was too late. I never thought she'd agree to take the plunge, without the old skeleton's consent, but when I told her I had a priest all lined up and waiting at a little church just around the corner, she just laughed that wonderful silvery laugh of hers. 'O.T.,' she said – she always calls me O.T., after the first two letters of my name – 'you are the *end*.' Whereupon Desie and I hopped into a waiting gondola and were rowed up to the church steps, where the candle-light was reflected in the water's edge. Venice is *the* place for getting married!

Her old man will be real sore, of course, but we had to get it done fast. The rumour is I'm going to get a posting abroad, to one of the Venetian empire's trouble spots, and Iago told me I oughtn't to risk leaving Desie. 'You never know who might catch her eye,' he said. 'Mike, for example. You know how fond she is of him.'

I laughed. Mike Cassio is the last person who could ever break up our relationship. He's the guy who carried secret notes between Desie and me when Desie's father got paranoid and wouldn't let her out of the house. Mike is the nicest guy you ever met. Working for the government, like me. Tipped for one of the best jobs in the empire – governor of Cyprus. Hope he gets it. One of the best guys around.

*   *   *

2 JANUARY

I still don't believe it. Desie and I had just got back from the wedding, late at night, and we were drinking champagne with Mike, who of course was our best man, when a message came that I was wanted at once at headquarters. My stomach clenched, because it sounded bad. In Venice, if they call for you in the middle of the night, nobody's going to see you again for a good long while, except the secret police and their jailers.

But when the official gondola had dropped me at the Doge's palace, everyone was all smiles. And five minutes later, I knew why. It's *me* they've chosen to be governor of Cyprus, and Mike is to be my number two. I just don't believe it.

Neither did Desie's old dad, when he turned up at the palace to accuse me of abducting his daughter. But it was OK. Desie had come along with me and she told them the truth – how she'd been in love with me ever since she heard the story of my escape from slavery. The Doge told Desie's dad that our marriage was perfectly legal, and he agreed that Desie could come with me to Cyprus and strut her stuff as the governor's wife!

Her dad nearly choked when he heard that.

A wonderful night, though just before we finally fell asleep I heard Iago whispering in my ear: 'Don't think they've picked you because you're the best man for the job. It's only because of your skin. They want a black guy in a top job, to show how liberal they are. But the moment you put one finger wrong, you'll be out, and Mike – the man they really want – will have your job.'

I paid no attention. Iago is always saying that sort of thing.

*　　*　　*

10 FEBRUARY

Cyprus is heaven. The governor gets a real castle to live in. Desie loves that, and the big four-poster bed in our room, and the view of the sea. The locals have welcomed us newlyweds to their hearts. Mind you, things got off to a good start. A storm got rid of the Turkish fleet that had been menacing the island for months. Now we just

guard the harbours, with half a dozen of our gun-
boats, and the Cypriots can get on with producing
that scrumptious lamb and red wine they serve
Desie and me with every night. This is *the* place!

Talking of the local wine, I'm afraid Mike had
too much of it the other night. He was drinking
with a bunch of young officers, before they all
went on guard duty, and somebody seems to have
picked a fight with him, and he lashed out with
his sword. The goddamned fool. It left me no
choice but to demote him, strip him of the
deputy-governorship.

'Don't do that,' whispered Iago, 'or you'll be
storing up trouble.' But rules are rules, and griev-
ous bodily harm (because I'm afraid Mike slashed
the fellow's face very nastily) has to be punished.
I had to take off his insignia and reduce him to
the rank of a junior, in front of all the guard.
Desie was watching, too, though she shouldn't
have been there. 'She dotes on Mike,' Iago whispered to me. 'She'll not forgive you.' I paid no
attention to his mutterings.

*   *   *

Iago was right, though. That's the maddening thing. He always has been, ever since he started murmuring to me when I was about five or six.

Do you have a voice that sometimes tells you, quite secretly, that things aren't what they seem? That your best friend doesn't like you as much as you like her? That your boyfriend is cheating on you? That your girlfriend really fancies someone else? That your parents only *pretend* to admire your drawings, or your music, or your football-playing, and they're really sniggering about you behind your back?

I reckon most of us have heard that sort of voice now and then. Some of us even give our voices names, as if they were real people.

Well, they *are* real. I don't mean we believe there are other people talking in our heads, the way people do when they go insane. We know it's just a part of ourselves. But it can be so powerful. You can have your life all sorted out and be clear of all trouble, and suddenly that little voice starts whispering: 'Why be so uptight? Be cool, have a good time, even if it does mean breaking a few rules.' That's the hardest sort of voice to say 'no' to.

I can cope when Iago says that sort of stuff to me. (I gave my voice a name, Iago, years ago – I found that made it easier to answer it back.) I can say 'no' when Iago tells me to freak out and have a wild time. I've got discipline. You have to have discipline to get where I've got. But when the voice starts whispering to me, 'O.T. –' yes, it calls me O.T. too – 'O.T., don't you wonder what so-and-so really *thinks* of you?' then it's hard not to listen.

Well, this time Iago was right enough. Scarcely a morning or afternoon goes by without Desie asking me if I won't reconsider my demotion of Mike. 'It wasn't his *fault*,' she keeps saying. 'You know what soldiers are like – someone spiked his drink. Give him another chance, O.T. Don't tell headquarters, just give him back his uniform and let him get on with the job. I've known Mike all my life, O.T., he's always been my best friend, you can't *treat* him that way.'

'I have to,' I said heavily. 'It's the rules.' In fact it was very difficult to say anything to Desie, because Iago kept chattering away. 'Sure he's her best friend. They were going to get married till you came along. Now she knows she made a mistake. You mark my words, she's cheating on you, behind your back.'

I laughed aloud at this. The idea of Desie cheating on anyone is just crazy. 'No one's ever seen such an honest girl,' I told Iago. 'She couldn't deceive anyone if she tried.'

'Oh, no? So why did she cheat on her father, tell him she was going to have an early night in bed, and then slip out of the back door to get married without his consent?'

I bit my lip. This was true.

'She's never had the hots for you,' went on Iago. 'She'd have married Mike if he'd been willing to elope with her. But he was too honest, he wouldn't hurt her old man. So she picked on you, just to get away from her dad. And now she's free, it's Mike she wants. Can't you hear?'

I told him to shut up. But at that very moment, Desie was saying: '*Please*, O.T. Be generous. You know how much Mike means to me.'

Something snapped in me. 'You bitch!' I screamed, and slapped her hard across the face.

She reeled back, touching the red place on her

cheek with her fingers. 'O.T.,' she whispered, 'what's the *matter*? This isn't you.'

I started to sob. I'd never hurt her before. I'd never been able to imagine that I could. 'I'm sorry,' I gasped. 'It was just a bad voice talking inside me. Go to bed. I'll come upstairs very soon.'

She had taken out a handkerchief and was dabbing her cheek with it. Tears were mixing with the blood. 'All right, O.T.,' she whispered. 'Don't listen to bad voices, just be your own sweet self.'

Something caught my eye. 'Your handkerchief,' I said. 'That's not your handkerchief.'

When we first started going out together, I had given her a handkerchief, a special one, a family heirloom. My mother had once been given it by a gypsy, a wise woman, and it had always brought luck. There were patterns on it. Desie always used it, washing it every night and hanging it out to dry in the bedroom. But now she was dabbing her cheek with a plain white handkerchief.

'I'm sorry, O.T.,' she sobbed. 'I didn't want to tell you. Your handkerchief has gone missing. I left it under my pillow, but in the morning it was gone.'

'We'll search for it, my sweet,' I said. 'I expect

it's under the bed. Now, you go up, and I'll be with you in half an hour, when I've dealt with all these letters that need answering.'

She went up and I started on the paperwork. Or tried to.

For a long while, Iago said nothing. He didn't need to, because my mind was full of just one word: handkerchief.

How *could* she lose it? It made no sense. Our bedroom is furnished very simply. Just the big bed, and a cupboard for clothes, and the window looking over the sea. Nowhere for things to get lost.

The clock ticked on. I was very, very tired. I shut my eyes, just for a moment – and saw it! I saw the handkerchief. It was in Desie's hands. She was tying it around someone's eyes, as a blindfold. And I knew whose.

Yes, Mike's, of course. They were in our bedroom and she was blindfolding him. Now he was chasing her around the room. He caught her and they fell together on to the bed.

I opened my eyes. 'It was just a dream, of course,' said Iago.

'It was horribly real,' I said.

'Dreams don't mean anything,' said Iago. 'You don't *know* she's given the handkerchief to Mike. You don't *know* they're having an affair. You don't *know* their plan is to goad you into doing something silly, so that Mike gets the governorship.'

'Silly?' I said. 'What sort of silly?'

'Like you did tonight, only worse. Next time, you won't just hit her, you'll strangle her, and Mike will burst in, just in time, and rescue her, and put you under arrest, and you'll lose everything. Your wife, your job, your reputation, your freedom. You'll spend the rest of your days as a guest of the Venetian prison department. What a great ending to a glorious career.'

'OK, OK,' I said. 'I'll just say nothing, do nothing.'

'That's right,' said Iago. 'You just leave Desie and Mike to have their affair behind your back. Don't let it get in the way of your career. There's lots of guys have made that decision.'

'Or,' I said, 'there's a third alternative.'

'Yes,' agreed Iago. 'There is. But you're not tough enough for that.'

Oh, yes, I am. Look.

Doesn't Desie look beautiful?

You don't stop looking beautiful when you've been smothered.

Strangling leaves nasty marks. Smothering doesn't do any damage.

She looks so beautiful now. And she'll never cheat on me again.

And Mike forgot their plan. He never burst in on us, to stop me killing her.

So I did.

There are tears on her cheeks.

I would wipe them if I had something to wipe with.

Ah, *there's* something I could use.

Just peeping out from under the bed.

A handkerchief. *Our* handkerchief.

Oh.

Oh, my God.

Oh . . .

If I kill myself with this knife, then I will have managed to kill Iago too.

I have to kill him.

Because it was all his fault.

As You Like It

FOR ONE WEEK ONLY!
We present
A JOLLY MUSICAL COMEDY
ARDEN DAYS

*with book, music and lyrics
by Billy Shakespeare*

SCENE ONE

Overture: lots of nice, jolly, tinkly tunes. Then the curtain goes up on some cut-out trees, with a park bench in front of them. On the bench are the Duke, who's wearing a dressing gown and a panama hat and smoking a cigar, and Jaques, a gloomy-looking man in a dark suit and bowler hat. The rest of the very small stage is filled with jolly young people in tennis clothes. Everyone except Jaques sings and dances happily.

EVERYONE:

> Arden, come to Arden!
> Give up your own back garden,
> And run away for a year and a day,
> For life's all play, we just make hay,
> We never work, oh nay, nay, nay!
> No need your heart to harden,
> For life's so jolly and we're never
>   melancholy
> In the spiffing old Forest of Arden.

DUKE:

I say, Jaques old man, why aren't you singing?

JAQUES:

I don't see what there is to sing about. You're supposed to be the Duke, but your wicked brother Frederick has kicked you out of your dukedom.

DUKE:

Yes, jolly nice of him. It means I can lounge about here all day, instead of being frightfully busy doing dukish sorts of things. It's much more pleasant here than at my ducal court, don't you think? Anyone for a swim? (*He takes off his dressing gown to reveal a striped bathing costume.*)

ONE OF THE JOLLY YOUNG PEOPLE:

No thanks, Dukey, we're all going to play tennis. Are you coming for a game, Jaques?

JAQUES (*gloomily*):

Not me. And I do wish you'd stop singing those jolly songs.

DUKE:

Oh, thanks for reminding us. Let's have another chorus before we go.

EVERYONE (*to Jaques*):
>Arden, good old Arden!
>We really beg your pardon,
>But it's so much fun here in the sun,
>That we feel our life has just begun.
>We can swim and play and run, run, run.
>No need to bring a bard on,
>For we'll think of a new rhyme every time
>In the sunny old Forest of Arden.

(They all run off, leaving Jaques sitting gloomily on the bench.)

SCENE TWO

The sitting room of a smart town house. Orlando, a good-looking young man in cricket flannels, is talking to his cross-looking brother Oliver.

ORLANDO:

I say, Oliver, I do think it's beastly of you not to give me any money. When Father died, he said in his will that you were to look after me, give me a good education and let me have my share of his money. And you haven't done any of that.

OLIVER:
Just go away and stop nagging me, Orlando.

ORLANDO:
You never let me go to university and I haven't got a penny. But I might make some money in the wrestling contest they're holding at court tomorrow. There's a big prize for the winner. I'm off to practise my wrestling holds. (*He goes.*)

OLIVER (*thoughtfully*):
A wrestling contest? Hm, I have a wicked idea.

(*Frederick, a villainous-looking man, comes in.*)

FREDERICK:
Hello, Oliver. Did I hear you say 'wrestling contest'? I've just passed that weedy-looking brother of yours in the passage and, do you know, I think he's going to enter for it.

OLIVER:
That's right. Golly, how Orlando infuriates me.

There's nothing so irritating as having a brother.

FREDERICK:

I couldn't agree more. Why don't you kick him out of the house, the way I kicked *my* brother, the Duke, out of his court?

OLIVER:

I've got a better idea. Why don't we arrange for Orlando to be beaten up in the wrestling match? If he had a few bones broken, that should stop him being such a pest about money.

FREDERICK:

Aha, that's a clever notion. You see to it right away.

(They sing:)

OLIVER AND FREDERICK:
>Brothers are a curse,
>Brothers are a pest,
>They're always getting worse,
>They're never at their best.
>We don't know why we hate them,
>It's simply that we do,

We want to see the back of them –
Well, wouldn't you?

Brothers, brothers, brothers, brothers,
Far more trouble than fathers or mothers.
Best to send them packing, best to wipe
   them out,
You'll be better off without them, there's
   no doubt.

Brothers are a pain,
Brothers are an ache,
They're never right as rain,
They're always on the make.
We don't know why we loathe them,
Or why they make us blue,
We want to see the end of them –
Well, wouldn't you?

Brothers, brothers, brothers, brothers . . .
   [etc.]

(They dance off, grinning wickedly.)

SCENE THREE

The lawn outside the ducal court. A crowd has gathered to watch the wrestling match. Among it are two pretty girls in summer dresses, Rosalind and Celia.

ROSALIND:

Oh, Celia, isn't it a lovely day?

CELIA:

Yes, and you ought to be enjoying the sunshine in the Forest of Arden with your father, the Duke, and his friends. I can't think why you stayed behind when *my* father kicked him out of his dukedom.

ROSALIND:

My Uncle Frederick was certainly very horrid to do that to Daddy. But I couldn't leave you, Celia, my poppet. You're my very best chum.

CELIA:

And you're my only friend at court, now that all the nice people have gone off to the forest with your father. Oh, here comes *my* father now.

(Frederick enters, with Oliver and his court wrestler, Charles, a huge ugly man in striped boxer shorts.)

FREDERICK *(whispering in Charles's ear)*:
You won't forget, will you?

CHARLES:
No, my lord. You want me to break both his arms, his legs, his nose and – I've forgotten how many ribs.

FREDERICK:
All of them, you elephantine athlete. Ah, here he comes now.

(Orlando enters, also in wrestling gear.)

Well, boy, are you ready?

CELIA *(to Rosalind)*:
I say, quite yummy, isn't he?

(Rosalind is transfixed by the sight of Orlando and can't manage to say anything.)

FREDERICK:

In the first contest of the afternoon, Charles the Crusher takes on Orlando!

(He rings a bell, and Charles and Orlando begin to wrestle.

Rosalind starts to sing.)

ROSALIND:
> It must be the sunshine
> That shines up above,
> That's making me feel
> As if I'm in love.
> But I've never seen
> Such a beautiful boy,
> I'm captured. Oh, rapture!
> My heart's full of joy.
>
> Is it love?
> No, it's just the summer weather.
> Is it love?
> No, it must be the heat.
>
> Is it love?
> No, it's just the summer lightning.

Is it love
Makes my heart miss a beat?

The temperature's climbing,
And here am I rhyming –
To see you is awfully pleasant.
This summery weather
Has brought us together,
And darling, I'm just incandescent!

Is it love?
Well, it can't be just the sunshine,
Yes, it's love,
Summer love,
That makes my life at last complete.

*(While she sings, Charles has been throwing Orlando
about like a rag doll. Suddenly, Orlando sees
Rosalind.)*

ORLANDO:
What a divine girl!

*(Inspired by the sight of her, he picks Charles up
effortlessly, holds him high in the air, then throws him
to the ground with a tremendous crash.*

Rosalind and Celia cheer, but Frederick is furious.)

FREDERICK:

Get up, you useless heap of flesh. You're supposed to have done that to him!

(Charles doesn't move. Frederick turns to Orlando.)

And as for you, you'd better make yourself scarce. Otherwise your brother here (*turning to Oliver*) will make things pretty hot for you.

(Oliver nods. He and Frederick and the crowd leave.)

ORLANDO:

Don't worry. I'm not hanging round here. I'll go off to the Forest of Arden. (*He exits.*)

ROSALIND:

Oh, don't go so quickly! (*Crestfallen.*) Celia, whatever am I to do? I've fallen desperately in love with Orlando.

CELIA:

Quite simple. Disguise yourself as a boy and pursue him to the forest. I'll come with you.

ROSALIND:
But why on earth should I disguise myself as a boy?

CELIA:
Because this is a musical. Come on! (*She sings*:)
> Arden, off to Arden!
> And if Dad puts a guard on,
> We'll creep away at dead of night,
> You in trousers – what a sight!
> And all the wrongs will soon be right.
> We'll live off bread with lard on,
> Yes, we two charmers will dress up as
>   farmers
> In the funny old Forest of Arden.

(They dance off happily.)

SCENE FOUR

The forest. Orlando is sitting on the park bench.

ORLANDO:
I was crazy to come here. I should have stayed

and let Frederick and my brother do their worst to me. Just as I was wrestling I caught sight of a most marvellous girl. They told me she's called Rosalind. And now I'm *here*, and she's *there*. And all I can do is think of her. In fact, I've written a song about her. (*He takes it from his pocket and sings*:)

> Rosalind,
> To my heart her name is pinned.
> Rosalind,
> And with mine her soul is twinned.
> She's as pretty as the whisper of a wind,
> Is Rosalind.
>
> Darling Ros,
> Oh, I love you, dear, because,
> Dearest Ros,
> You're the wizard of my Oz.
> Oh, I fell for you the moment that you
>   grinned,
> My Rosalind.
>
> Your name isn't easy to rhyme with,
> Even Shakespeare would find it hard.
> But dear, you're the one I chime with,
> So I send this Valentine card.

Lindy sweet,
Will you change your name to mine?
Life's complete
If you'll be my Valentine.
You're the freshest fruit, and other girls
   are tinned,
  My Rosalind.

(*Sighing:*) I'll pin the song to a tree. Not that *she* could ever see it – she's miles and miles away.

(*Enter Rosalind, in a school cap, blazer and shorts, with Celia, who is wearing a space alien mask.*)

ROSALIND:
Gosh, Celia, I can't walk another step. We must have done at least fifty miles.

ORLANDO:
That voice – it's her! (*Seeing Rosalind:*) Oh, no, it isn't, it's a schoolboy. What's your name, my little fellow?

ROSALIND (*whispering to Celia*):
That face – it's him! (*To Orlando, in a deep voice:*)

I'm Ganymede, but you can call me Jimmy for short.

ORLANDO (*seeing Celia*):
And who – or rather, *what* – is your friend?

ROSALIND:
She lives in a flying saucer. She's called Aliena. It's the female version of Alien.

CELIA:
Beep-beep!

ROSALIND:
We're completely lost. (*Seeing the song pinned to the tree*:) Ah, maybe this will tell us where to go.

(*Enter Jaques, looking as gloomy as usual.*)

JAQUES:
It certainly won't. (*To Orlando*:) I'm extremely cross with you, young man. I happened to be standing behind a gooseberry bush while you were singing your little ditty, and now you've

defaced a perfectly good tree by pinning your rubbish to it.

ORLANDO:
But I'm in love with a girl called Rosalind –

ROSALIND (*in her own voice*):
Gosh! (*In her Ganymede voice:*) I mean, how soppy.

ORLANDO:
And I want to tell the world, even the birds and the bees, the hedgerows and the trees, how much I adore her.

JAQUES:
In love? Bah! There's no such thing. It's just a piece of acting, like the rest of life. (*Sings:*)

> All the world's a stage,
> A play we have a part in,
> You think you've lost your heart in
> This scene.

> All the world's a script,
> A book of jokes and verses,

Of broken hearts and curses –
It's mean!

First you're a baby, then a schoolboy,
Acting wild and tough.
Fine while it lasts, so play it cool, boy,
The going gets more tough.

Soon the curtain falls.
Time to stop pretending.
If there's a happy ending,
Hooray!
But who can say what's waiting
On the next page of your play?

ROSALIND (*to Orlando, in her Ganymede voice*):
Excuse me, did you say you were in love with
someone called Rosalind?

ORLANDO:
That's right. I worship the ground she treads on.

ROSALIND (*examining the ground beneath her feet*):
Do you? Well, perhaps I'd better give you some
lessons in how to woo her. Would ten o'clock
tomorrow morning suit you?

ORLANDO:
Perfectly. (*He goes off, whistling 'All the world's a stage'.*)

ROSALIND:
Whoopee!

(*She takes Celia's hands and starts dancing up and down with glee.*)

JAQUES (*gloomily*):
Why does everyone have to be so merry? (*He goes off.*)

SCENE FIVE

The forest, next morning. Oliver and Frederick are searching among the trees.

OLIVER AND FREDERICK (*singing*):
    Brothers, brothers, brothers, brothers,
    Far more trouble than fathers or mothers.
    We will send them packing, we will wipe
       them out,

We'll be better off without them, there's no doubt.

OLIVER:
Yes, but I can't find *my* wretched brother Orlando anywhere. (*Spotting the song pinned to the tree*:) Ah, this is his handwriting – I'd know it anywhere.

FREDERICK:
I'm sure *my* wretched brother the Duke is somewhere around. I'll try this path. (*He goes off.*)

OLIVER (*reading the song*):
'You're the freshest fruit, and other girls are tinned.' What rubbish!

(*Celia enters, holding her alien mask.*)

CELIA:
It's not rubbish, it's very beautiful.

OLIVER (*seeing her*):
Jumping jellybeans! *You're* very beautiful, you mean.

CELIA:
Oh! (*She pops on her mask.*) Beep-beep!

OLIVER:
Take that silly thing off. You're the loveliest girl
I've ever set eyes on.

(*Rosalind enters.*)

ROSALIND:
He's late.

OLIVER:
Who is?

ROSALIND:
Orlando. I'm supposed to be giving him a lesson
in wooing. Wait a minute. Aren't you his wicked
brother?

OLIVER:
I used to be, but now I've met this beautiful girl,
I'm going to become a reformed character.

CELIA:
I say!

More Shakespeare Without the Boring Bits
(She allows Oliver to embrace her.

The Duke wanders in, in his swimming costume.)

DUKE:
Hello, everyone! What are you doing here, Rosalind?

ROSALIND:
Daddy, you're not supposed to recognize me. I'm disguised as a boy. But it's lovely to see you again!

(She hugs him.)

ORLANDO *(entering)*:
Did someone say 'Rosalind'? *(Sees Rosalind.)* I say, I must have been rather shortsighted yesterday. Er, will you marry me?

ROSALIND:
Of course. Then we can all live happily ever after.

JAQUES *(entering)*:
It won't last, I tell you! There's bound to be something nasty round the corner.

FREDERICK (*entering and seeing the Duke*):
Brother!

JAQUES:
I warned you. Here comes the something.

FREDERICK (*to the Duke*):
I mean you no harm, brother. I was intending to murder you, but I've just met an elderly clergy-man who has convinced me of the error of my ways. You can have your dukedom back. I'm going to stay here in the sunshine, in the Forest of Arden.

DUKE:
We all are!

(*The chorus enter in their tennis clothes and all dance and sing:*)

ALL:
>Arden, we love Arden!
>This day's a lucky-starred one,
>We'll stay for ever in the sun,
>For we know our life has just begun.

And we're all in love, yes, everyone.
It's time to bring this card on –

(Jaques raises a large card which reads 'The – Happy – End'.)

ALL:

So we hope you've had a wonderful time
In the sunny old Forest of Arden!

King Lear

17 MAY

Dear Mum

Thanks so much for your postcard. It feels years since I've seen you. In fact it *is* years now – I suppose about three years since you went to Australia. It's lovely that it's all worked out so well for you.

I'm never sure whether you want news about Dad. I think usually you don't, but there *is* rather a lot I want to tell you about him at the moment, so here goes.

I know you found him utterly impossible, which was why you went off to Australia, and until now I have to say I thought you were absolutely and completely wrong about that. He's always been utterly gorgeous to me – madly generous, always asking my advice about everything, and being terribly nice (and not at all the jealous father) when Frank and I got engaged. So I was very happy to go on living at home until the wedding came around.

Of course it did make things a bit difficult between me and the Uglies. I think it was Dad who first made up that name for them – the Ugly Sisters – when they were two gorgeous-looking little twins in the pram. Of course, I wasn't born then, so the name was just a harmless joke. But when I came along and Dad started doting on me, I know they did sometimes feel a bit miffed, and calling them the Uglies wasn't quite so much of a joke, because honestly, Mum, the way they behaved to me was a bit ugly sometimes. No worse than older sisters usually behave to a younger sister, I suppose, but when they became teenagers they began to be nasty about Dad behind his back, and I couldn't stand that. I longed to go and tell him, but he was scarcely ever at home in those years – he was always in London, making pots of money, as you know.

It's the money that's upset things now, I'm afraid. Dad kept telling me that, with my wedding to Frank coming up, he wanted to change his will. I do wish he wouldn't talk like that, but you know what an awful show-off he's always been about his money, and how he's always been telling me and the Uglies that we wouldn't be short of a penny when he died. As if we cared – at least, I don't.

Anyway, the trouble blew up the night before the wedding. The Uglies had come to stay, of course, bringing their husbands, so we were quite a merry party. At least I thought we were going to be.

After supper, Dad asked us all to come into his study. (I forgot to say, Frank was with us too, of course.) He sat us down and then said he was going to talk about his will. 'I have to tell you,' he said in a solemn, pompous voice, 'that I am a very rich man indeed.' I started to giggle – I always do when he talks like that – and Frank pinched me to stop me, because Dad was taking it all very seriously.

'Since I have three daughters,' Dad went on,

'the obvious thing is for me to divide everything into three equal parts.' I glanced at the Uglies. They weren't giggling. Goneril was smiling quietly to herself – she's always been the greedy one, so I suppose she was just thinking of all that cash – and Regan was wearing her usual sour expression – probably resenting the fact that anyone else was going to get any of it (that's Regan all over). Honestly, I don't know how they found such decent husbands. Sorry, Mum, I mustn't start getting bitchy – but they have been pretty foul to me over the years.

'Three equal parts,' Dad repeated. 'But then again, I asked myself, *Why?* As you know, I've made all my money in the very competitive world of business, where the best man wins and the rest lose. So why should I just hand it all over to you without giving you the chance to compete for it?'

I froze. There was a look in Dad's eye that told me he was in one of his batty, crazy moods. He'd been perfectly all right all evening, but now I could see he was hyping himself up. You remember those moods, don't you? Well, of course you do – it was what finally drove you away. For days or weeks or months, Dad would be bounding

around like a two-year-old, giving everyone pre-
sents and inventing wild schemes, and you'd have
to try to calm him down. Then he'd get into a
frightful black depression and not say a word to
anyone for ages, except to tell us how sorry he
felt for himself. Well, that evening I could tell we
were in for a wild mood.

And what did he mean by 'competition'? Some
sort of party game?

'What I want,' he said, 'is for each of you girls
in turn – first Goneril, then Regan, then you,
Cordelia, to tell me how much you love me.'

That sounded pretty crazy to me, but I was
waiting for the next bit.

Then I realized there wasn't going to be a next
bit. That was it: we each had to tell him how
much we loved him.

'And the winner is the one who says she loves
you the most?' I laughed. 'Come on, Dad, be serious. What's going on?'

'I'm perfectly serious,' he growled.

'Dad, you're barmy,' I said. 'You're making it
like an *auction*! I've never heard anything so hor-
rible in my life.'

Dad went purple in the face. 'If you don't like

it, you can leave,' he shouted. 'But don't think you'll get a penny from me if you do. Come on, Cordelia, you can at least say, "I love you, Dad." That won't hurt you, will it?'

I couldn't believe what I was hearing. I got to my feet. 'If you behave like this, Dad,' I shouted, 'I don't love you. I don't love you at all.' And I stormed out of the room and went up to my bedroom in floods of tears.

Frank came upstairs about half an hour later, looking pretty grim. 'That was a very nasty charade,' he said. 'Your sisters went through with it. Goneril told him he was the most adorable Daddykins in the world, and Regan laid it on pretty thick too. They're both giggling about it now in the kitchen, over a fag and a glass of whisky.'

'Dad didn't take them seriously, did he?' I asked. 'He can't be that stupid.'

'I'm afraid he did. He's split all the money – and the house – equally between the two of them. And they won't even have to wait till he's dead. He's giving it all to them now, so they won't have to pay a huge amount of tax when he dies. Plus the house – he's selling it, because it's worth such an enormous amount, and he'll go and live with them. And I'm afraid, dearest Cordelia, you're going to get nothing at all.'

'I couldn't care less,' I said, 'as long as I've got you. But I suppose you won't want to marry me now I'm penniless?'

'Darling Cordelia,' said Frank, kissing me, 'if you think I was going to marry you for your money, you're even madder than your father.'

So that's how we stand at present. Frank and I are going to live in France, the way we always planned, and Dad's going to divide his time between Goneril and Regan. I hope they'll all be very happy together.

Poor old Dad. I'm awfully afraid he's going to wake up and realize he's made a terrible mistake. But I hope not. I still love him, in spite of the way he's behaved to me – I could tell from his mad-looking eyes that it was just one of his moods.

I'll pass on any more news when I get it, Mum. Frank and I had a very quiet wedding without any of the family, and we're just off to France now.

Lots and lots of love
Cordelia

*   *   *

10 OCTOBER

Dear Mum

I'm frightfully worried about Dad. I'm sending on a letter I've just received from Goneril. To be fair to the Uglies, things obviously haven't been easy for them. But they still can't treat Dad like this. Let me know what you think.

Lots and lots of love
Cordelia

Dear Cordelia

Regan and I feel that we should write to you about Father. We have reluctantly taken the decision to put him in an old folks' home.

As you know, the arrangement was that, after selling the house, he would spend half the year with each of us. That sounded fine in principle, and Regan and I were both looking forward to six months of his company, followed by a gap so we could get on with our own lives. Unfortunately it didn't work out that way, even from the start.

The first problem was that he'd forgotten to make any arrangements for his furniture and, would you believe it, the most enormous movers' van rolled up here at eight o'clock in the morning on the day he was supposed to be arriving. I've never seen so much stuff. Well, I had seen it, of course – we were brought up with it all – but Regan and I have our own homes now, carefully furnished, and we really couldn't fit more than a very few items into our houses. We had to tell him to put the rest in store. He was terribly upset about that, but this was nothing to what came next!

On his first night with me and my family, I discovered that he'd organized a dinner party for twenty of his friends! I say 'organized', but all he'd done was invite them, and leave me to arrange the meal! Of course, I told him he could do no such thing – he could have a couple of people to supper *if he asked me first*, but I wasn't running a restaurant for his benefit. At which point he started shouting to me about ingratitude – how I ought to be so grateful for all the money he'd given me – and then he yelled that, if I wouldn't look after him properly, he'd go straight off to Regan and never darken my doorway again. So I let him ring for a taxi and off he went.

Of course, the same thing happened when he got to Regan's. She had the same row with him about the furniture, and once again he tried to invite a whole bunch of friends to the house without asking her, and I'm glad to say she was as firm as I'd been. But as he'd burnt his boats with me, he had to stay there for a bit. Regan got on the phone to me and we agreed that the thing was *to be firm* and not give way to his ridiculous demands. We could see that he was starting to go downhill – indeed, this whole business of giving everything away to us and rejecting you, Cordelia (who'd always been his favourite), was a pretty clear sign that he was going senile. And the one thing you've got to be with senile old people is *firm*. Then they know where they are.

In fact, Father *doesn't* seem to know where he is. He's taken quite a turn for the worse since he arrived at Regan's – she says he gets up in the middle of the night and wanders around the house, muttering to himself about ungrateful daughters. So Regan and I have reluctantly started looking at old people's homes, and we've found one that should suit him very well. Of course, the fees are going to be very expensive, and if you and Frank felt you could make a contribution, that would be splendid. I know that Regan and I have all Father's money, but we want to put most of it in trust for our children and honestly, Cordelia, it was your own silly fault that you didn't get a penny.

I must stop – Regan has just rung me up to say that Father seems to have wandered off into the pouring rain in the early hours of this morning and hasn't been seen since. She's told the police.

Yours in haste,
Goneril

*   *   *

11 December

Dear Mum

Awful things are happening and I don't know who to turn to.

Dad is dying. Goneril lied to me. The place she and Regan had decided to put him was a mental hospital. When the police found him wandering about in a thunderstorm in his pyjamas, he was suffering from hypothermia and his mind had completely gone, so the mental hospital agreed to take him in at once. They put him in a locked ward, but he managed to escape with a couple of other patients – two wretched chaps known in the hospital as the Fool and Poor Tom – and the three of them roamed the countryside for weeks. Now Dad's been found, there isn't much life left in him, I'm afraid – he sits up in bed muttering quite happily to himself, but the doctors say he won't last long. (I'm writing this by his bedside.)

Meanwhile, I'm frightened about the Uglies. Frankly, they're madder than Dad now. They're obsessed with the idea that Frank and I want their money, and they think we're going to attack them. Frank came over from France with me when there was the panic about Dad, but he's had to go back, and I'm on my own now and frightened of what they may do to me. There's an awful story going round that they've attacked some old friend of Dad's and actually *blinded* him because they thought he was on my side. It can't be true, but

there's certainly something very nasty going on and, oh, Mum, I'm *frightened*.
                              Cordelia

                    *   *   *

Dear mother-in-law

I have some terrible news. Cordelia has been murdered. Her sisters were convinced she was after their money – greed had made them quite insane.

Cordelia's father found her body and the shock of it killed him.

Goneril and Regan are dead, too – Goneril poisoned Regan and then killed herself. Good riddance to them both.

Things have been more awful than you can imagine.
                              Frank

The Winter's Tale

Have You Got a
Personal Problem?
Are you in need of
Urgent Advice?
Consult the
DELPHIC ORACLE,
the world's favourite Agony Aunt.
Instant replies at low cost.

Phone/fax 000 999 000. E-mail HELPLINE@DELPHI

Dear Delphic Oracle

I have a tricky problem. My husband, Leontes, invited an old school chum to stay and we've all been having a nice jolly time for the last few weeks. But now Leontes has got it into his head that Polixenes (that's his chum) and I fancy each other.

He keeps pressing Polixenes to stay another week, but I know he can't wait to see the back of him. To make matters worse, we've just discovered that I'm pregnant – and Leontes thinks that Polixenes must be the father!

It's utterly absurd – I like Polixenes, but I don't fancy him, and we certainly haven't been having an affair. What on earth am I to do?

Yours anxiously

Hermione

PS Leontes has now got it into his head that our son Mamillius isn't his either. He keeps peering into Mamillius's face and saying he doesn't look like him. Naturally Mamillius gets a bit upset at this, and you can imagine what I feel.

*　　*　　*

Dear Hermione

What a tricky situation. Probably your husband is having some sort of mid-life crisis. My advice is, persuade his chum to go home as quickly as possible, then keep your fingers crossed till the baby is born. With luck, it will look exactly like your husband.

Yours sympathetically
The Delphic Oracle

* * *

Dear Delphic Oracle

I have an unusual problem. For many years I have been butler, cook and valet to a charming gentleman who wouldn't say boo to a goose. But lately he's changed altogether.

An old schoolfriend of his came to stay and after a while my employer began to behave very oddly.

Now he has asked me to poison his friend.

Should I report him to the police? I would hate to do this, as he has always been very good and generous to me. But if he thinks I'm willing to be a hit-man, he's seriously mistaken.

What advice can you give me?
Yours anxiously
Camillo

*   *   *

Dear Camillo

You should certainly not commit a murder on behalf of your employer. My advice is, leave your present job at once – and warn your employer's friend there's trouble in store for him if he hangs around a moment longer!

Yours understandingly
The Delphic Oracle

*   *   *

Dear Delphic Oracle

My life used to be peaceful and happy. Now everything seems to be going wrong.

My wife has been unfaithful to me with an old schoolfriend of mine. As if that wasn't bad enough, I can see very clearly that our son can't be my child at all – he doesn't look remotely like me. And now my faithful butler has disappeared in the middle of the night, along with my wife's lover. They are obviously all ganging up against me.

My wife says I am talking nonsense and it's all my imagination. But it can't be, can it?

Yours frantically
Leontes

*   *   *

Dear Leontes

Yes, of course, it can. Your wife is perfectly right. Stop talking nonsense or something worse will happen to you.

Yours reprovingly
The Delphic Oracle

*   *   *

Dear Delphic Oracle

I wonder if you can give me some advice? A friend of mine, Hermione, is having an awful time with her husband, Leontes. She was going to have a baby, and he became convinced it wasn't his – so he locked her up! He's really off his head. But now the baby has been born, it looks so much

122

like him that he ought to realize it *is* his child.

The trouble is, he won't come near it, so he hasn't seen the likeness. I've got a key to where Hermione is locked up, so I thought I could take the baby and bring it to Leontes and show him. But he's so crazy that he might do something awful to it. Do you think it's worth the risk?

Yours uncertainly

Paulina

* * *

Dear Paulina

You're right – it's a terrible risk – but nothing ventured, nothing gained.

Yours rather unhelpfully

The Delphic Oracle

* * *

Dear Delphic Oracle

Oh dear. It didn't work. He took one look at the baby and decided it looked just like his friend Polixenes. I thought he was going to kill it, so I took it away again quickly.

But he wouldn't let me take it back to its mother. He's persuaded my husband, Antigonus, to take it to a desert and leave it there, so it'll almost certainly die. This is awful! What on earth am I to do?

Yours distractedly
Paulina

*   *   *

Dear Paulina
Not much you *can* do, is there?
Yours cynically
The Delphic Oracle

*   *   *

Dear Delphic Oracle
Can you help me? I have been living in this desert for fifteen years and there is nothing left to eat. Should I pack up and move?

Yours hungrily
A Large Bear

*   *   *

Dear Large Bear

Don't move. Wait a couple of days and a chap called Antigonus will be turning up with a baby. Don't eat the baby – there's not enough meat on it to give you a decent meal – but Antigonus should provide a good few mouthfuls.

Bon appetit!
The Delphic Oracle

*   *   *

Dear Delphic Oracle

I am a shepherd, living near the desert, and I am fed up with looking after sheep. The one thing I like in life is babies, but there aren't any here. Should I move to town and get a job in a crèche?

Yours lonelily
A Sad Shepherd

*   *   *

Dear Sad Shepherd

Stay exactly where you are. There is a baby on the way. Keep a careful look out and you will spot it. It will be lying on a rock, near where a large bear is eating a man.

Yours encouragingly
The Delphic Oracle

*　　*　　*

Dear Delphic Oracle

How on earth did you know? It is a very nice baby, a girl, and I have called her Perdita, which means 'Lost One', as I suppose somebody must have lost her.

I will give her a good home.

The bear sends a message: 'Thanks for the excellent meal.'

Yours delightedly
A No-Longer-Sad Shepherd

*　　*　　*

Dear Delphic Oracle

It's me again.

My friend Hermione's husband, Leontes, is behaving just as badly to her. He let her out of her prison – just so he could scream abuse at her. Please could you send him a note telling him that none of the things he imagines are true?

Yours hopefully
Paulina

PS My husband never came back from taking the baby to the desert.

*   *   *

Dear Leontes

As I've told you before, you're talking nonsense. Your wife has never been unfaithful to you. The baby she had was yours. Your old schoolfriend had done nothing wrong. Your butler was blameless too. You're crazy to be jealous, so come to your senses or (as I warned you before) *something worse will happen.*

Yours threateningly
The Delphic Oracle

*   *   *

Dear Delphic Oracle,

You're talking rubbish. Keep out of what doesn't concern you. I *know* I'm right.

Yours furiously

Leontes

*   *   *

Dear Delphic Oracle

Something awful has happened. Leontes, my friend's mad husband, had just torn up your letter to him, the one that said something worse would happen if he didn't come to his senses, when – it did!

The boy Mamillius, whom Leontes was convinced wasn't his son, had been very miserable when his mother was locked up and he developed a nasty disease. Now, someone rushed in to say he'd died!

Leontes turned pale and said that this was your warning coming true – so you must be right after all. He'd been making a terrible mistake.

Of course, he was terribly upset about Mamillius's death, while as for poor Hermione, she dropped to the ground, unconscious with the shock.

I decided to get her out of the place as quickly as possible, before Leontes could change his mind again and do her some harm. So now she's living secretly at my house (there's plenty of room, now that my husband has disappeared). I'm not sure whether she'll survive the shock. But I have a plan – which I am sending to you in invisible ink. Tell me what you think of it.

Yours secretly
Paulina

*   *   *

Dear Paulina

I think the invisible plan is excellent. Best of luck with it!

Yours approvingly
The Delphic Oracle

*   *   *

Dear Delphic Oracle

You won't know me, but sixteen years ago I think some friends of mine wrote to you about a nasty situation I was in — an old school chum of mine got it into his head that I had become his wife's lover. Anyway, that's all past history now, though it was terribly sad — his son died and his wife dropped dead of grief.

But what I'm writing to you about now is quite different.

I wonder if you can give me some advice? I'm a very well-to-do sort of chap and I had high expectations of my son, Florizel — he's tall, dark, handsome and terribly bright. But he's fallen in love with a shepherd's daughter — not at all the sort of girlfriend I wanted him to have. And he's determined to marry her. She's got quite a nice name, Perdita, but of course she hasn't a penny in the world.

Should I stop the marriage?

Yours parentally
Polixenes

*   *   *

Dear Polixenes

Don't do anything rash till you've had a look at this Perdita. If you don't want your son to

know you're spying on them, go in disguise.
        Yours all-knowingly
        The Delphic Oracle

*   *   *

Dear Delphic Oracle
  How right you were.

I disguised myself and went to the shepherd's house with my faithful butler, Camillo (he saved my life years ago, when my old school chum Leontes was trying to poison me — but that's another story).

Sure enough, there was my son Florizel, making a fool of himself (as I thought) with this shepherdess — you know, doing country dancing and all that sort of thing. I was furious, but Camillo had somehow spotted that Perdita, the shepherdess, wasn't exactly what she seemed and the next thing I knew, he'd told Florizel to take her off to — of all people — my ex-chum Leontes, whom of course I hadn't spoken to since the awful business sixteen years ago.

Would you believe it, Perdita turns out to be Leontes's daughter! And Leontes has been

131

perfectly sane, poor chap, since his son and wife died.

So of course I was absolutely delighted for Florizel to marry her. Couldn't be better, could it, though I wish poor Hermione was still alive to see her beautiful grown-up daughter happily married to my son.

But even clever old you can't manage that, can you?

Yours wistfully
Polixenes

*　　*　　*

Dear Polixenes
Who says I can't?
Yours slyly
The Delphic Oracle

*　　*　　*

Dear Delphic Oracle
Just to let you know that the plan I discussed with you, in invisible ink, sixteen years ago has worked.

Leontes was over the moon to find out that the baby he'd sent to the desert all those years ago had survived and had grown into a beautiful young woman – and was going to marry his friend Polixenes's son Florizel. But he kept saying how sad he was that Hermione hadn't lived to know it.

So I told him I had had a waxwork made of Hermione which looked just like her and the sculptor had just delivered it to my house. It wasn't too difficult to persuade him to come and see it.

When we took the covers off the waxwork, he just stared. 'It's unbelievably like her,' he whispered, 'except that she looks a lot older.'

'Ah,' I said, 'that's because I told the sculptor to make it look like Hermione would be *now*, if she'd lived another sixteen years.'

Very cautiously, Leontes went up to it and touched it – and jumped back. 'It's *warm*,' he said in astonishment.

'Yes, the wax isn't really dry and hardened yet,' I said. 'You must be very careful with it. By the way,' I went on, 'it's got machinery inside it, which makes it move.' And I pretended to press a button.

Whereupon the 'waxwork' stepped off its pedestal and put its arms round Leontes. And at last he realized that Hermione hadn't been dead at all, but had been living in secret with me all the time ... as you knew!

So now Leontes, who'd lost his child and his wife, has a child and a wife once more, and a second chance to be a good husband, which is probably more than he deserved; but if we only got what we deserved, we'd have fairly awful lives.

Anyway, I like happy endings, don't you?

Yours contentedly
Paulina

*   *   *

Dear Paulina
    You bet I do.

Yours misty-eyed
The Delphic Oracle